SAMPLE COLORING PAGES

FREE COLORING PAGES!

Check out: **SwearWordColoringBook.com** for
FREE swear word coloring pages.
Don't forget to sign up to my mailing list for news,
updates, and future FREE coloring pages!

Need EXTRA stress relief?

F-word Coloring Book for Adults

Coloring designs with the most popular swear word ever! Nothing but "f-words" and phrases with "f-words."

Available on Amazon! Just search **"F Word Coloring Book John T"**

Swearing Is Caring: Bold & easy coloring book

The cutest swear word coloring book in the world!

Available on Amazon! Just search **"Swearing is Caring John T"**

The FIRST dictionary of "sentence enhancers!"

GAG GIFT OF THE YEAR!

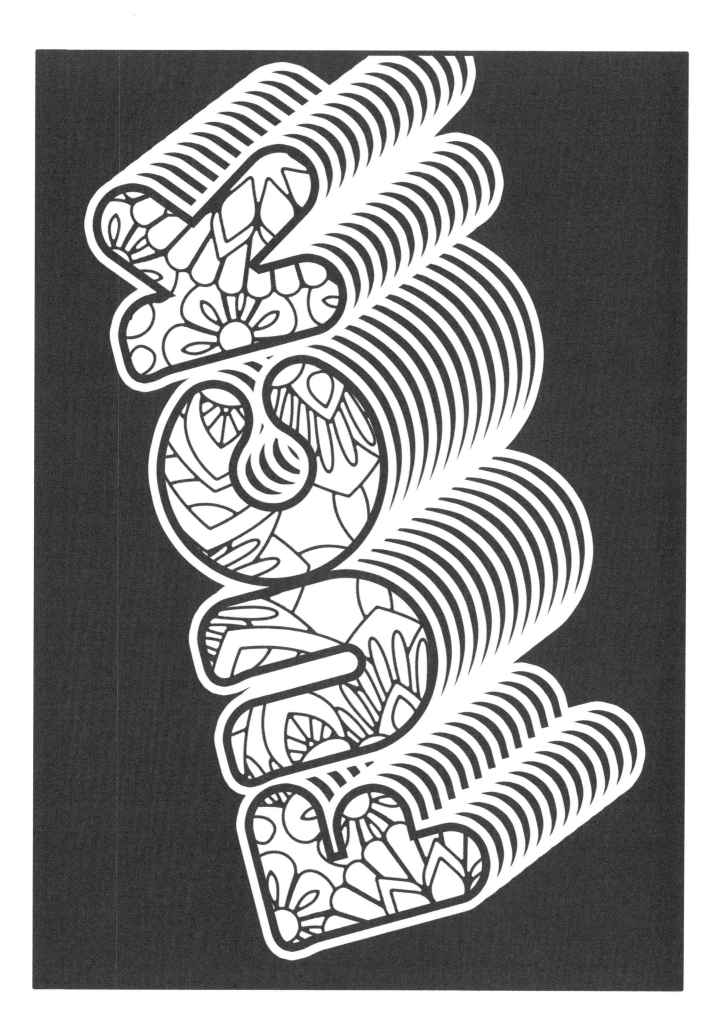

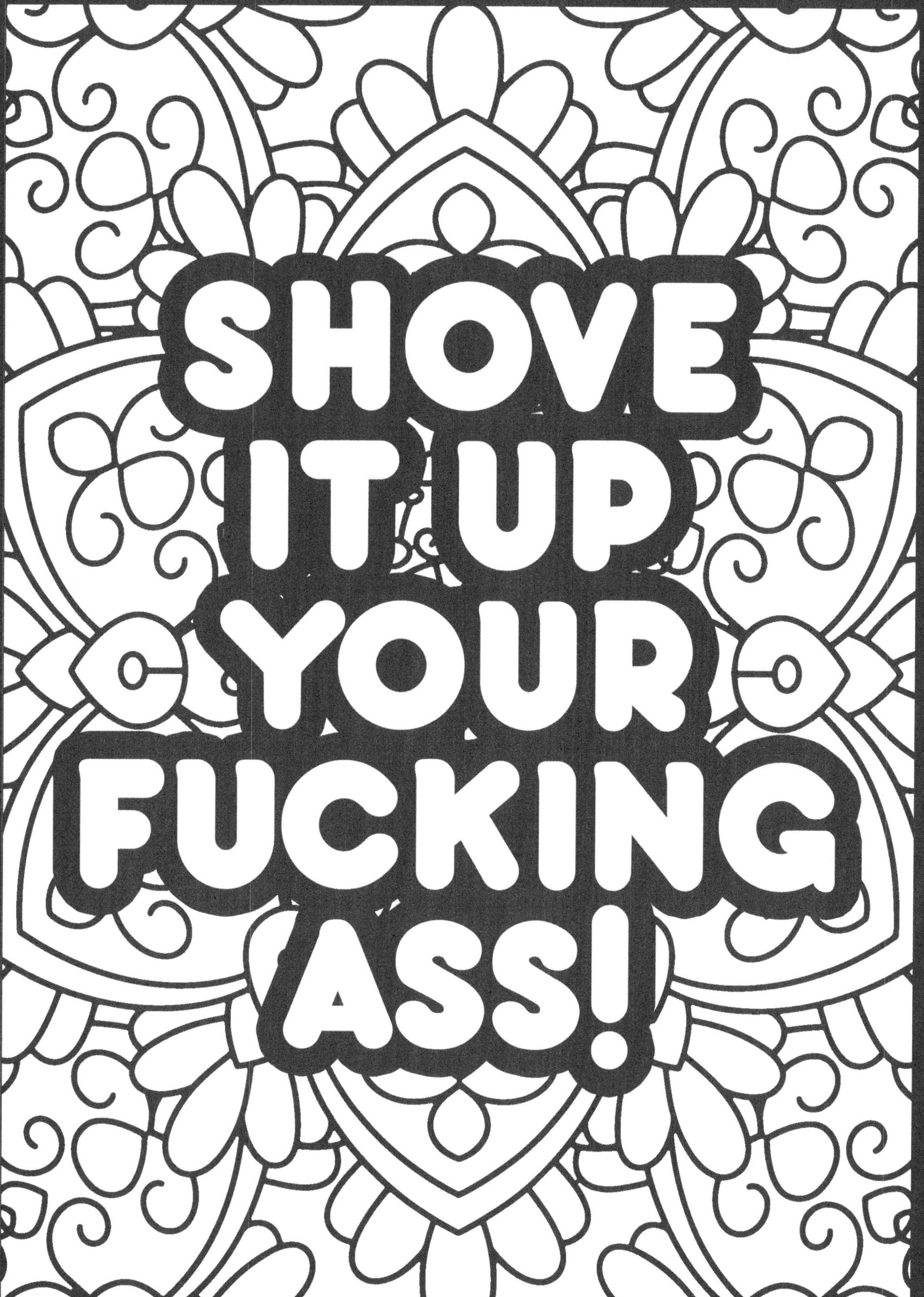
SHOVE
IT UP
YOUR
FUCKING
ASS!

TAKE A FUCKING CHILL PILL

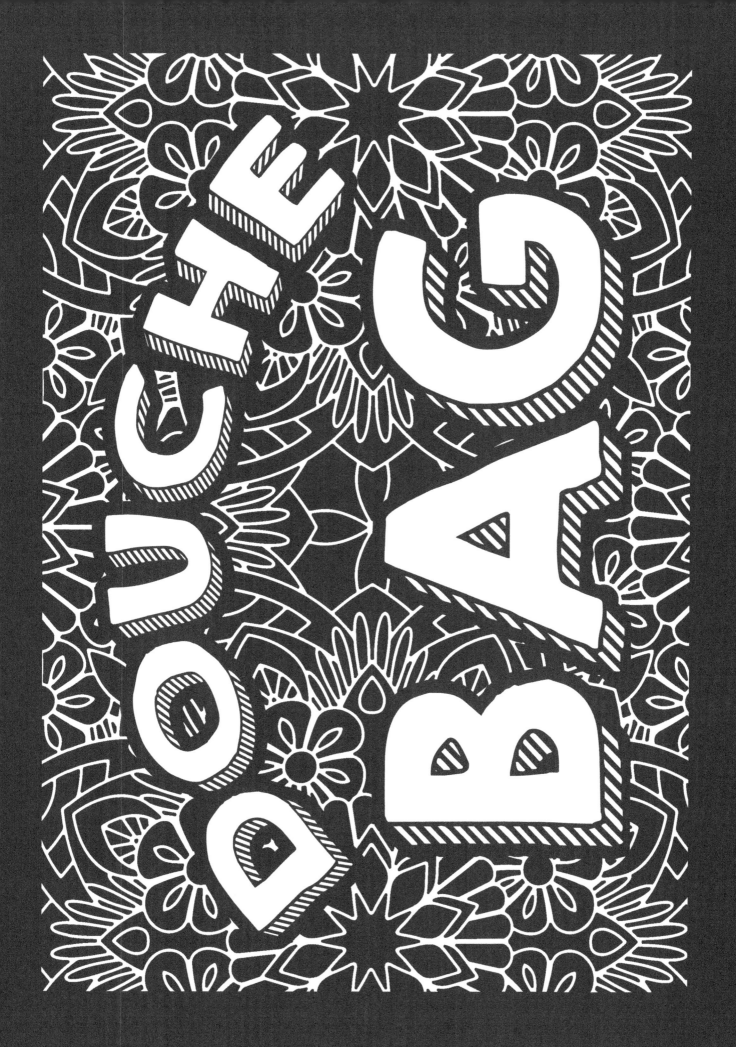

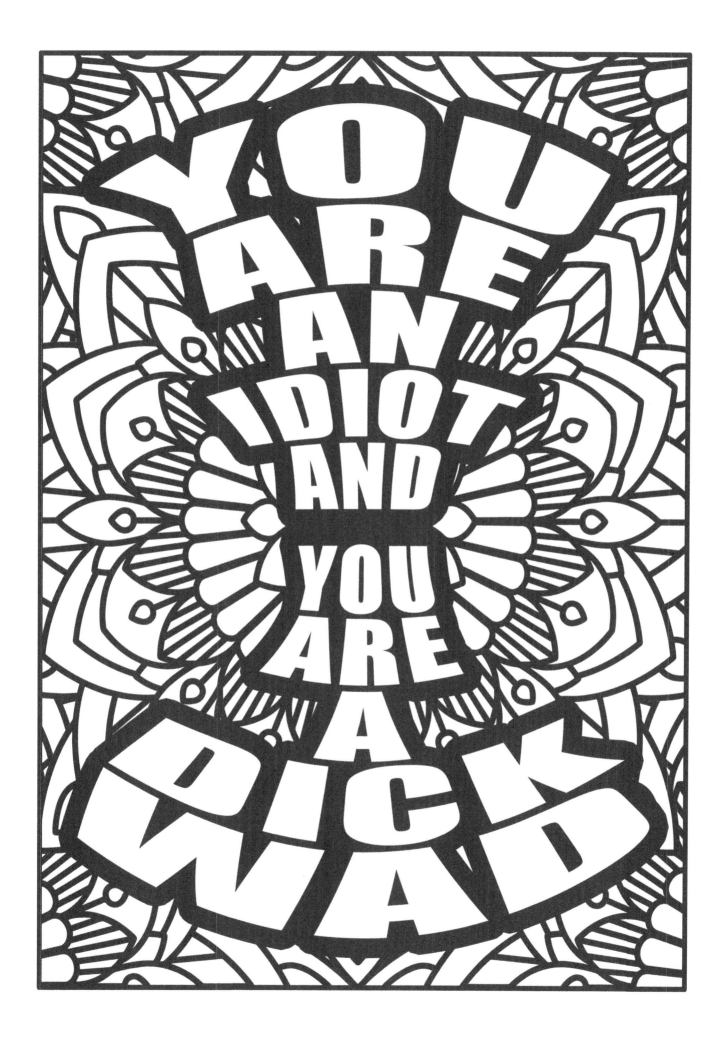

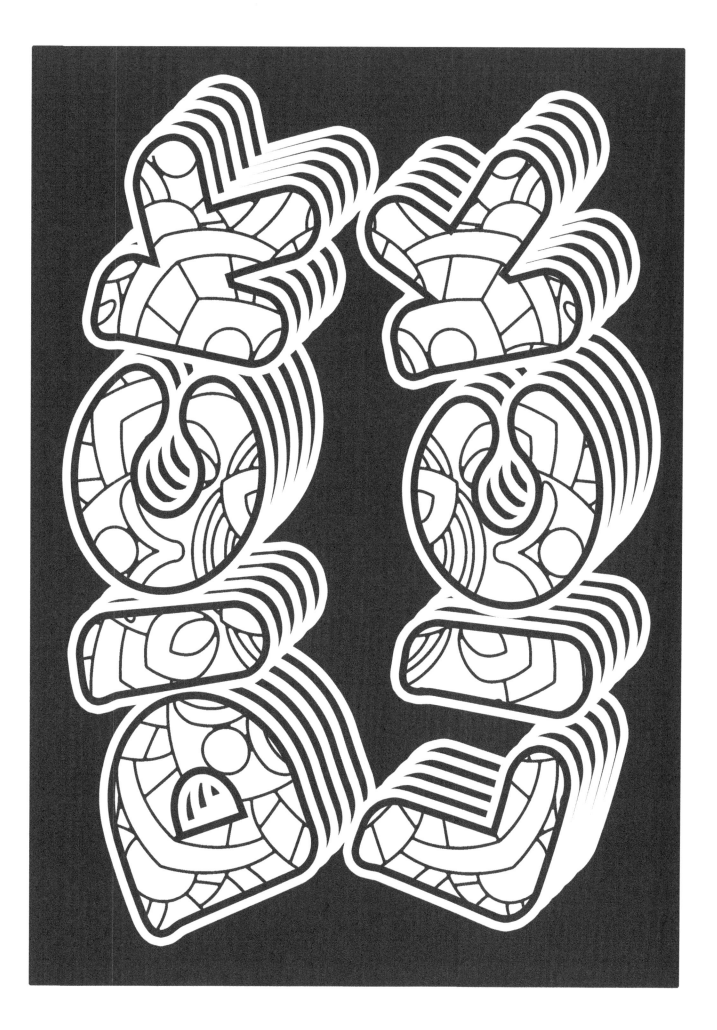

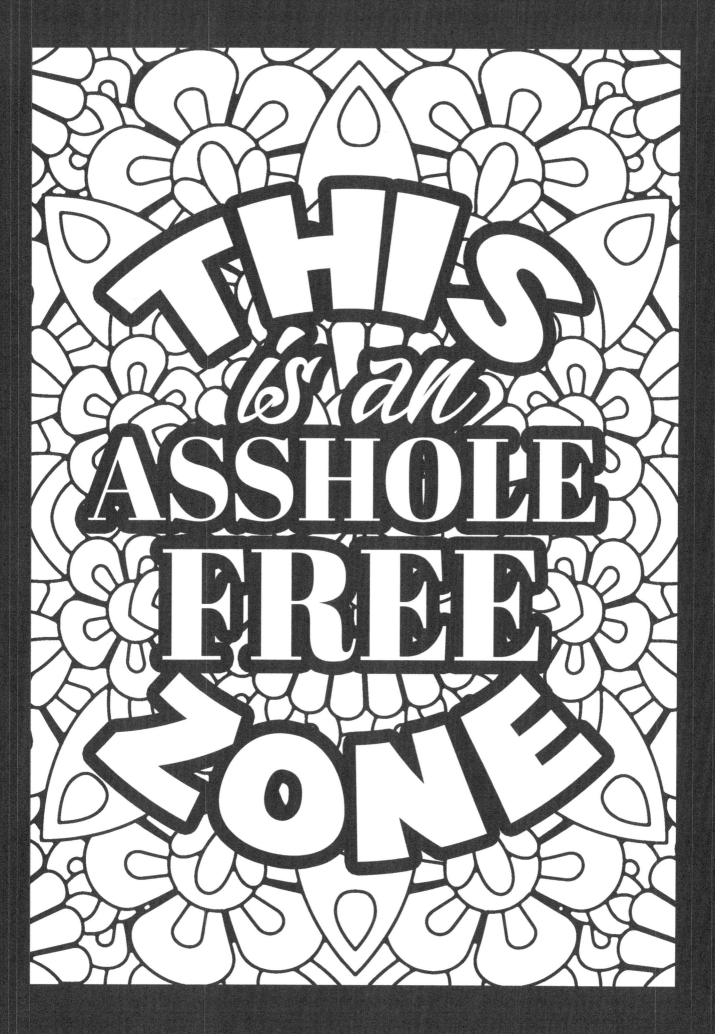

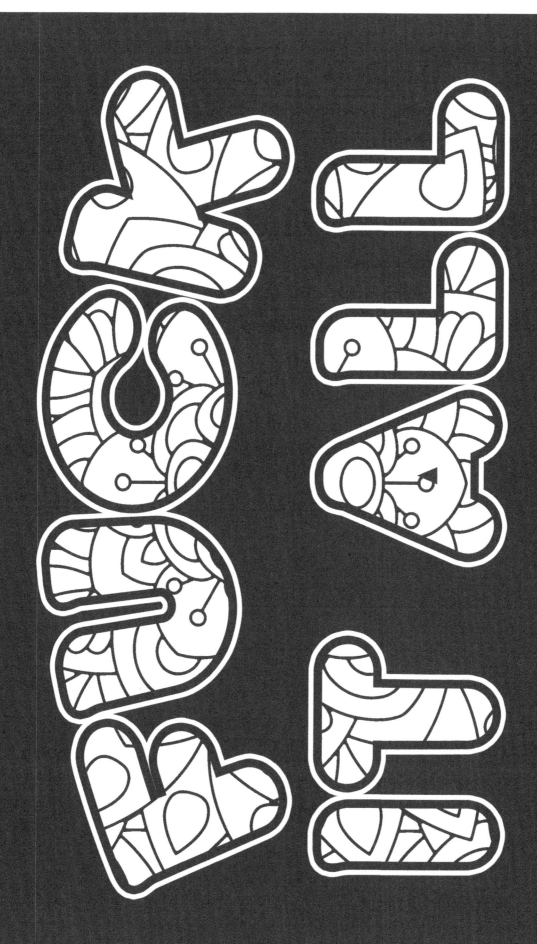

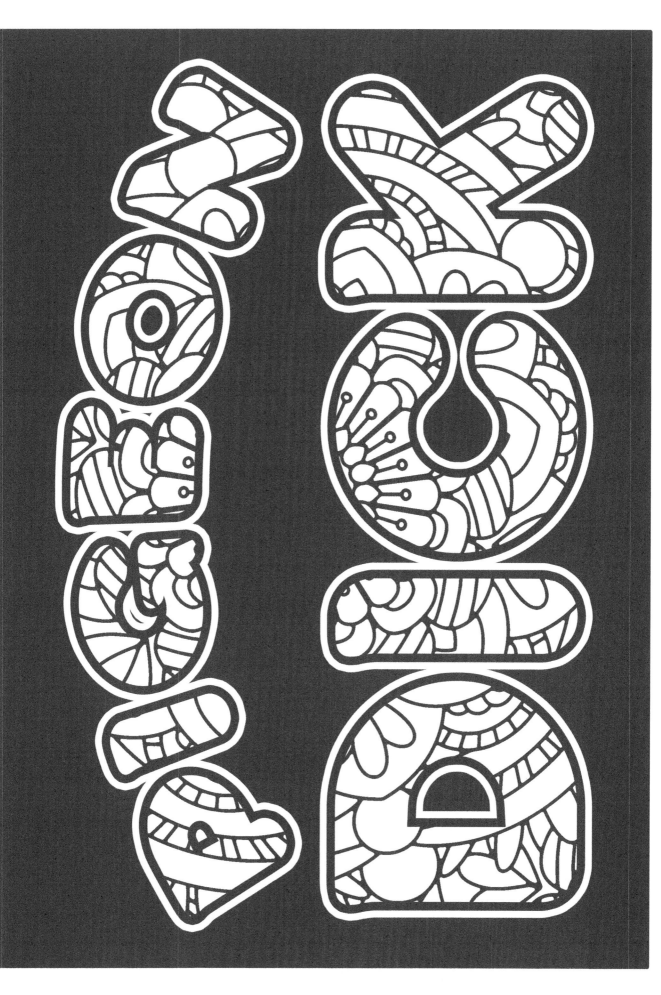

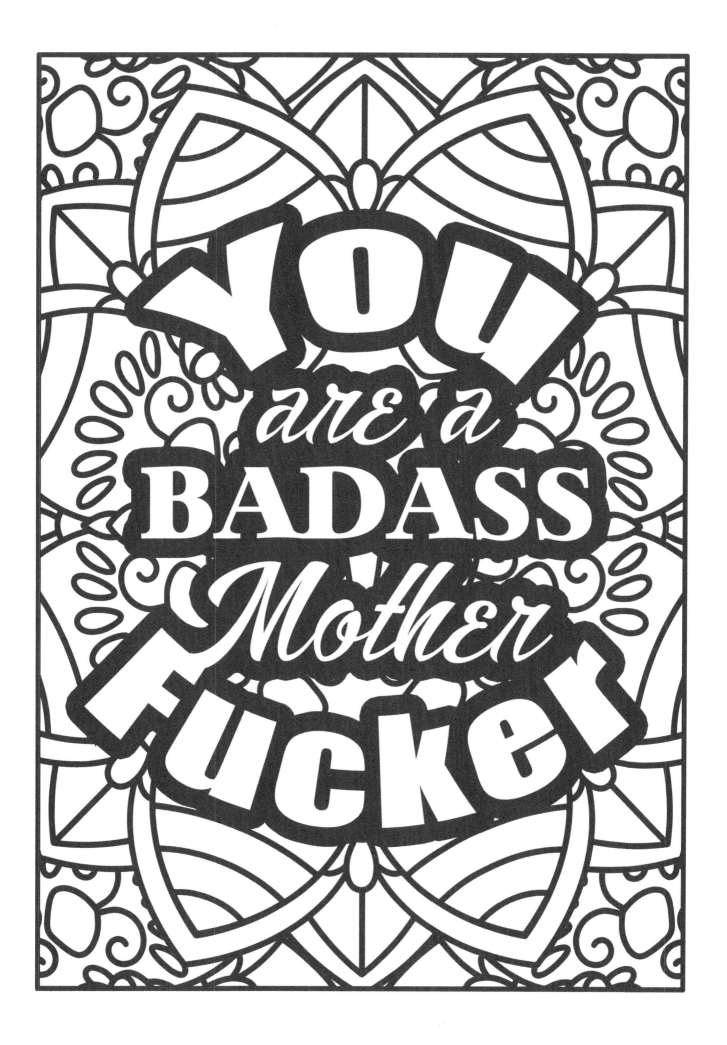

Made in the USA
Las Vegas, NV
16 November 2024

11942084R10031